NIGHT STORY

NIGHT STORY

By Ethel and Leonard Kessler

Macmillan Publishing Co., Inc., New York

Collier Macmillan Publishers, London

Macmillan Publishing Co., Inc.
866 Third Avenue, New York, N.Y. 10022
Collier Macmillan Canada, Ltd.

Printed in the United States of America

10   9   8   7   6   5   4   3   2   1

LIBRARY OF CONGRESS CATALOGING IN PUBLICATION DATA

Kessler, Ethel.   Night story.

(Ready-to-read)

SUMMARY: A truck driver on an overnight drive
observes the shifting scenes and moods of a night
filled with activity.

[1. Night—Fiction. 2. Night work—Fiction]
I. Kessler, Leonard P., date.   joint author.
PZ7.K483Ni 1981   [E]   80-24626   ISBN 0-02-750220-1

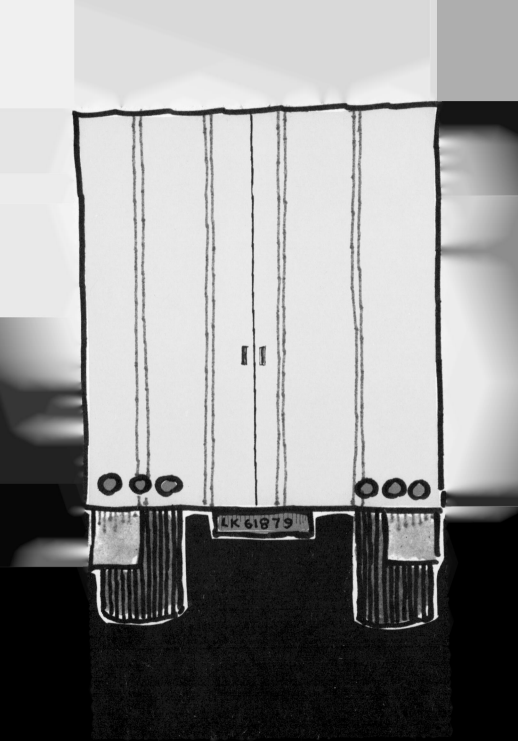

Night time.
Dark time.
Quiet time.

"Time to get ready
for sleep,"
says Mother.

On the farm
the cows,
the horses,
and the sheep
have all been fed.
Time for sleep.

In the hen house
the chickens rest
on their perches.
They shut their eyes.
Time to go to sleep.

In the woods
the crows
and robins
go to sleep
in dark trees.

The chipmunks scamper
into their holes.
They curl up
and go to sleep.

Night time.
Dark time.
Shadows all around time.

"Time to go to work,"
says Father.
"Time to drive my truck.
I drive at night!

"I see
things at night
that people don't see
in the day.
I see eyes
in the dark.

"Eyes see me.
Look out!
It's a skunk!

"I hear sounds
at night
that people don't hear
when they are asleep."

Whoo,
hoots the owl.
Whoo.
He turns his head
from side to side.
He is looking for food.
Night time is hunting time.

Chug-O-Rum,

Chug-O-Rum,

croak the hungry bullfrogs.

Green frogs and
brown toads
grunt and trill and croak.
Night time is eating time.

And night time is
working time.
Clickety-clack.
Clickety-clack.

The long freight train
goes by.
The engineer drives
at night.

Zooooom.
The plane blinks
across the black sky.
Pilots fly the jet
at night.

In tall buildings
the lights are on.
The office cleaners
work at night.
Empty the baskets.
Sweep and mop.
Wax the floors
with big machines.
Make the offices
shiny clean for the
next day's work.

179

A siren screams.
Lights flash.
Someone is hurt.
The ambulance crew
helps at night.

It's quiet
in the hospital.
But there is
work to do.

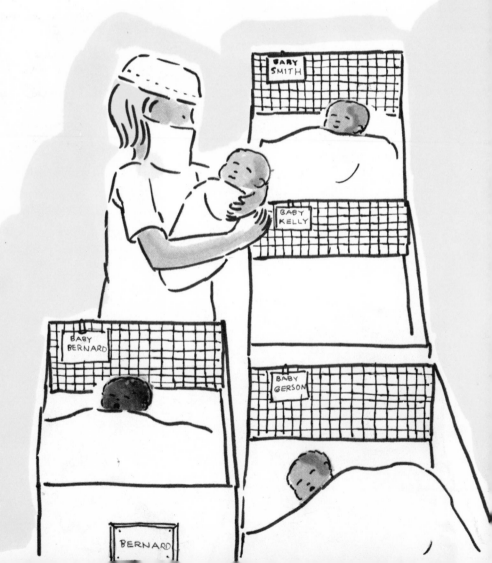

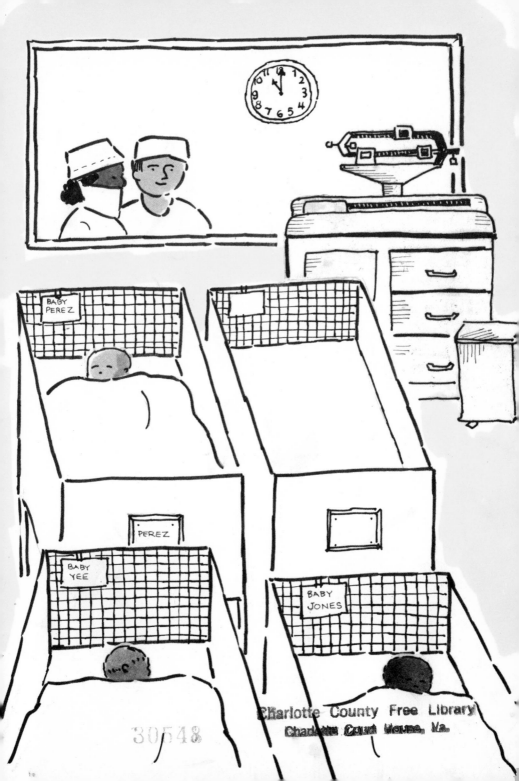

Hurry, hurry!
The ambulance is here!
Call the doctor.
Call the nurses.
The night shift
is on the job.

The wind blows down
an old tree.
It falls on the
power lines.
Elm Street goes dark.

Send out
the emergency crew.
They work through the night
to move the tree
and fix the wires.

Night watch.
Police officers
check the
empty stores.

Fire.
Fire!
Four alarm.
Fire and smoke
on the top floor.
Ladders go up.
Hoses splash.
Fire fighters
work at night.

Deliver the load.
Then on the road again.
Green flashing signal.
One toll booth is open.
The toll taker works
all night.

It's a long drive.
Two hundred miles,
and a hundred
miles to go.
Diner up ahead.
It's time to eat.

Hot coffee.
Hot soup.
Hot chocolate.
Hot sandwiches.
Scrambled eggs.
Night workers
eat at night.

Night sky.
Light sky.
It's daybreak.
Time to go home.

"It's time to get up,"
says Father.

"And time for me
to go to sleep."